Vaes, Alain
The wild hamster

DATE DUE

MR1 3 '96	JY1 4 '99	JY 2 '02	
1 3 '96	OC1 4 '99	SE 1 '02	
JY 8 - '96	SE 27 '00	AP 10 '03	
AG1 3 '96	JA 2 '00	JE 11 '03	
OC 28 '96	MR 18 '02	JY 16 '0	
OC 9 '97	AP 22 '02	AG 3 '04	
MR 2 - '98	JE 26 '02	AG 8 '0	
MR 16 '98	JY 9 - '02	AP 2 1 '0	
OC1 4 '99	JY 15 '02	JY 1 4 '09	

The Wild Hamster

Written and Illustrated by
Alain Vaës

Little, Brown and Company
Boston · Toronto

Written and illustrated by Alain Vaës
The Porcelain Pepper Pot
The Wild Hamster

Illustrated by Alain Vaës
The Steadfast Tin Soldier, by Hans Christian Andersen

First Edition

Library of Congress Cataloging in Publication Data

Vaës, Alain.
  The wild hamster.

  Summary: The inhabitants of a small village find a way to put their enormous, voracious hamster to good use.
  1. Children's stories, American. [1. Hamsters – Fiction] I. Title.
PZ7.V18Wi   1985   [E]   85-5260
ISBN 0-316-89504-0 (lib. bdg.)

DNP

Published simultaneously in Canada
by Little, Brown & Company (Canada) Limited

Printed in Japan

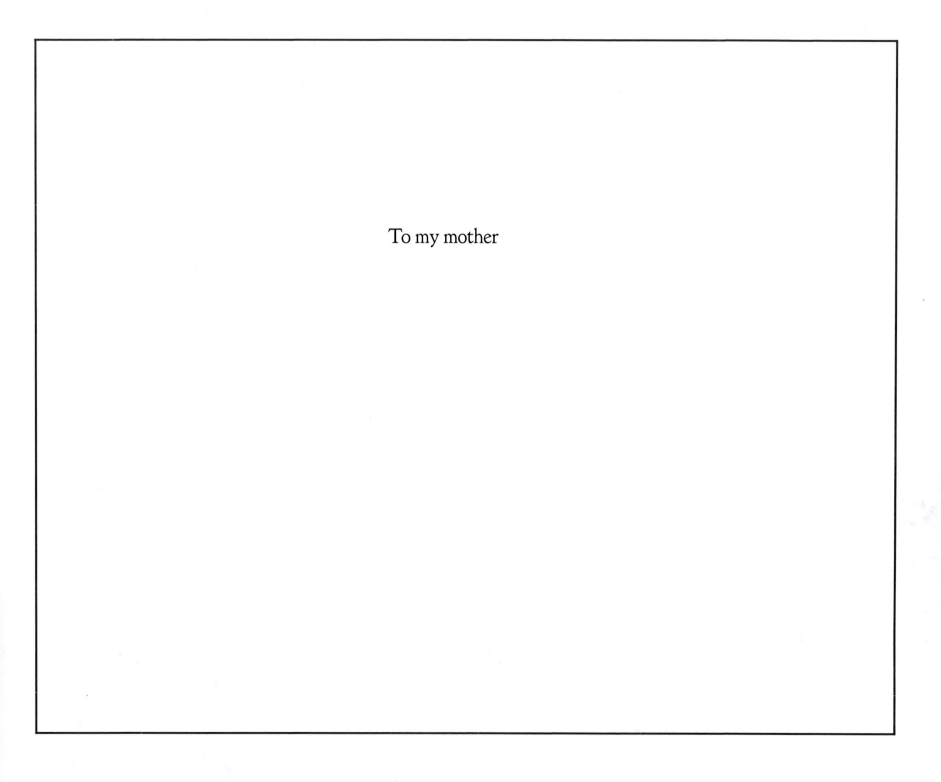

To my mother

Once upon a time, there was a peaceful village, surrounded by fields and orchards. On the edge of the village lived a farmer and his family.

One day the farmer's son and daughter went for a walk in the countryside and came upon a little mouselike animal. He was so small and frail that they decided to adopt him and bring him home. When the farmer and his wife saw the tiny creature they, too, wanted to take him in.

The children called him a "hamster" and built a small house for him in the kitchen. They also saw to it that his little bowl was always filled with grain and fresh vegetables.

The hamster was a sweet and affectionate pet, and he quickly became used to the house. The children loved playing with him. Even the cat and the dog seemed to accept him.

There was only one problem. The little animal was always starving, wanting more and more food. But the more food he ate, the bigger and fatter he got. He soon reached the size of a rat — then a chicken, then a pig!

The farmer was not rich, and feeding the hamster became a serious problem. The hamster continued to grow to extraordinary proportions, and eventually the farmer considered killing him. But the children wouldn't let him do away with their pet!

The farmer knew he had to do something, for the hamster had reached the size of a horse. The grain supply was dangerously low, and the other farmers, fearing for their crops, had threatened to take matters into their own hands.

In spite of his children's tears and protests, the farmer took the hamster out into the woods and abandoned it.

Peace was restored to the village. Everyone went back to work, and life was simple again. But one day, strange and alarming noises came from the forest. The hamster, by now the size of an elephant, was eating the bushes and trees!

The villagers were afraid that they would lose their forest and fields. So all the men formed an expedition, bringing along ropes, and a wagon pulled by strong horses.

By offering it food, the men captured the hamster and hoisted it onto the wagon to bring it back to the village.

The farmer's children were afraid that their beloved pet would be killed after all. But the villagers had a better idea for the hamster.

They built a huge wheel connected to a mill that, when turned, would grind grain for the whole country. The hamster took to the wheel right away, and soon made the villagers rich. Best of all – the exercise prevented him from getting any bigger!

Nowadays hamsters don't grow so big, but in memory of their illustrious ancestor, they still have a wheel to turn in their cages.